THE BEAR UNDER
THE STAIRS

HELEN COOPER

For Ted

Marks and Spencer plc
PO Box 3339
Chester CH99 9QS

shop online
www.marksandspencer.com

ISBN 978-0-5525-6694-0
Printed in China

William was scared of grizzly bears,
and William was scared of the
place under the stairs.

It was all because
one day he thought
he'd seen a bear,
there, under the stairs.

And he'd slammed the
door shut –
wham, bang, thump!

William worried about the bear.
He wondered what it might eat.
'Yum, yum,' the bear said,
in William's head.
'I'm a very hungry bear,
perhaps I'll eat boys for tea!'

So William saved a pear for the
bear who lived under the stairs.

And when no-one was watching,
William whipped out his pear,
opened the door,
threw the pear to the bear
that lived under the stairs,
then slammed the door shut –
wham, bang, thump!

William had kept his eyes shut tight,
so he didn't see the bear in its lair
under the stairs.

But he knew what it looked like!

And at night…

while William dreamed…

Every day, William fed
the bear that lived under
the stairs.

He fed it bananas, bacon and bread.

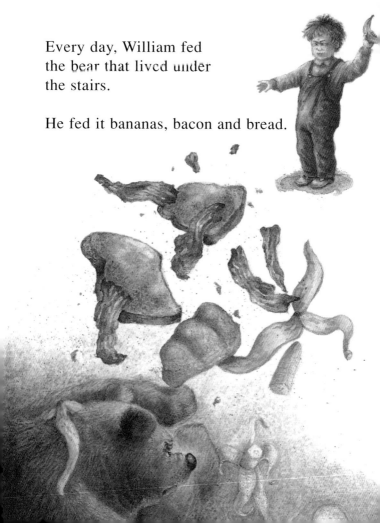

He fed it
hazelnuts,
haddock
and honey…

But he always kept his eyes
closed tight, and slammed the
door shut – wham, bang, thump!

After a while there was a strange smell,
in the air,
near the bear,
under the stairs!

The smell got stronger, and stronger,
until his mum noticed.
'There's an awful pong,' she said.
'I think I'd better do some cleaning.'

'No!'

screamed William, very scared.

'Don't go in there!'

Mum lifted William on to her lap.
'William, whatever's the matter?' she asked.
So William told her all about the hungry bear
in its lair, there, under the stairs.

Then William and Mum went to fight
the bear that lived under the stairs.
Brave William had his eyes wide open
all the time,
and when they opened the door,
he saw…

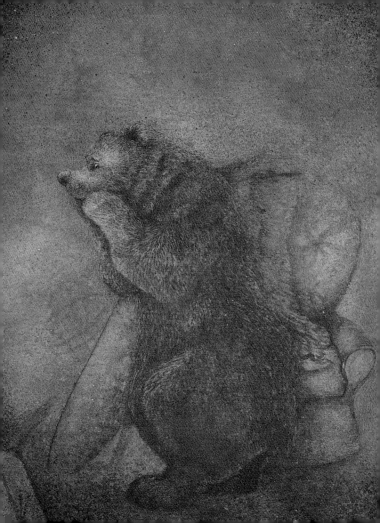

An old furry rug,
a broken chair,
no bear,
no scare,
and horrible stinky food everywhere!

So William and
Mum cleaned up.

Then they went shopping and
bought William a little brown grizzly
bear of his own. It had such a nice face
that William was never scared of bears...

... ever again...